For Justin and Lizzy,
who don't shy away from
the rainbows or the clouds

SIMON & SCHUSTER BOOKS FOR YOUNG READERS
An imprint of Simon & Schuster Children's Publishing Division
1230 Avenue of the Americas, New York, New York 10020
© 2023 by Jessie Sima
Book design by Lizzy Bromley © 2023 by Simon & Schuster, Inc.
SIMON & SCHUSTER BOOKS FOR YOUNG READERS and related marks are trademarks of Simon & Schuster, Inc.
For information about special discounts for bulk purchases, please contact Simon & Schuster
Special Sales at 1-866-506-1949 or business@simonandschuster.com.
The Simon & Schuster Speakers Bureau can bring authors to your live event. For more information
or to book an event, contact the Simon & Schuster Speakers Bureau at 1-866-248-3049 or
visit our website at www.simonspeakers.com.
The text for this book was set in ITC Lubalin Graph.
The illustrations for this book were rendered in Adobe Photoshop.
Manufactured in China
1222 SCP
First Edition
2 4 6 8 10 9 7 5 3 1
CIP data for this book is available from the Library of Congress.
ISBN 9781665916981
ISBN 9781665916998 (ebook)

Weather TOGETHER

JESSIE SIMA

Simon & Schuster Books for Young Readers
New York London Toronto Sydney New Delhi

Nimbus and Kelp were from different worlds.

One was from the sky,

one was from the sea,

but they became friends
in the space in between.

When they were together, things were all sunshine and rainbows.

At least, they seemed to be for Kelp.

YAY!

For Nimbus, on the other hand,
things were sometimes . . .

a little bit . . .

cloudy.

Nimbus had grown up surrounded by clouds,
but this one was different.

She thought about talking to her new friend about it,
but she didn't want to cast a shadow on the fun.

And there was *plenty* of fun to be had on land.

Enough that no one seemed to notice
Nimbus's occasional shift in weather.

Nimbus didn't know why she couldn't be sunny all the time.

It seemed so easy for everyone else.

She tried pretending the cloud wasn't there.

She tried running from it.

She tried bottling it up.

But the more Nimbus tried to get rid of it, the bigger
and more noticeable the cloud became.

It grew

and grew

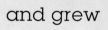

until something small

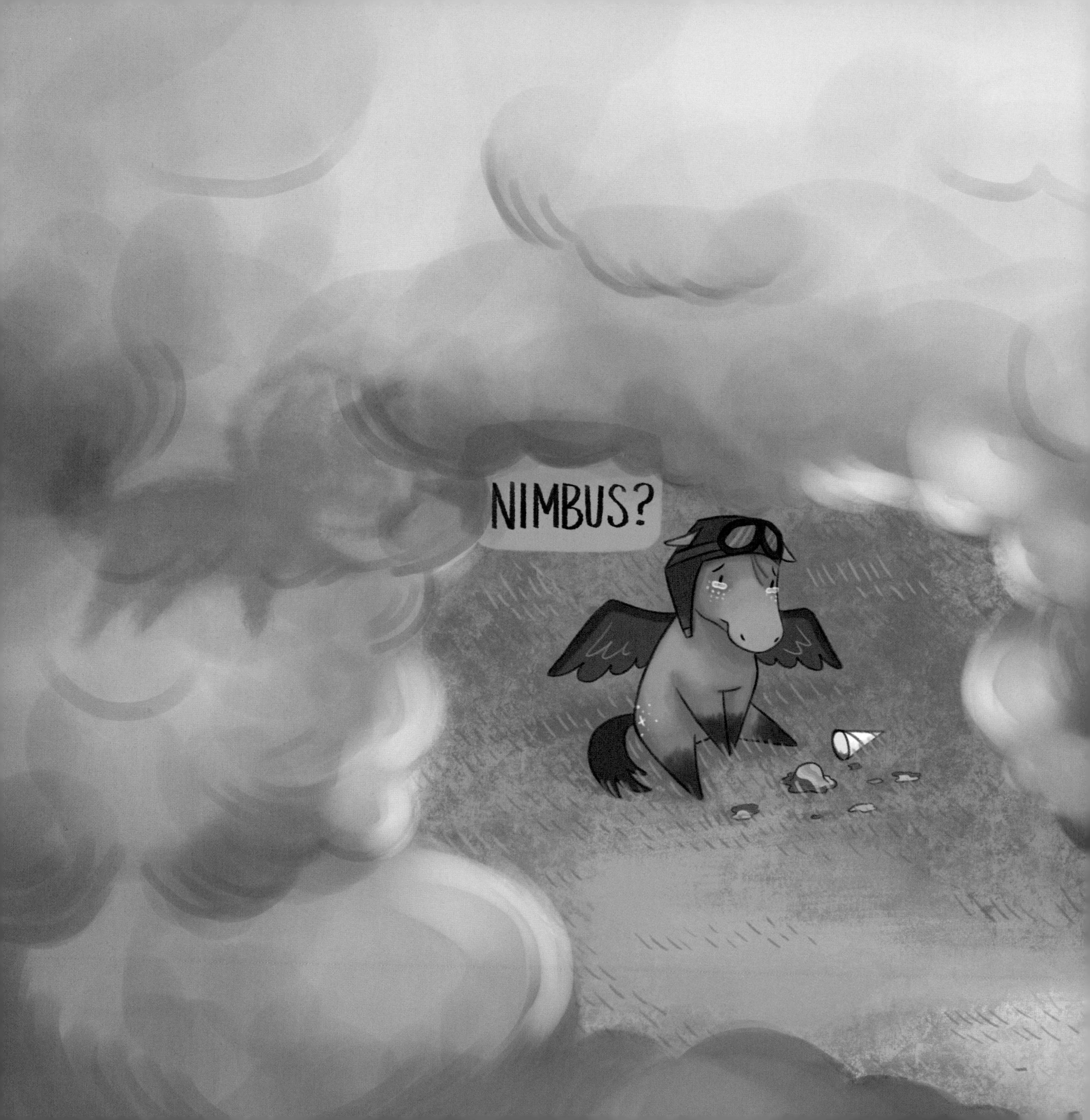
NIMBUS?

The storm that had been brewing
finally burst forth.

And this time . . .

it seemed like *everyone* noticed.

COME BACK!

Nimbus flew away as fast as she could,
which was very fast indeed,
hoping to find a place where all eyes
would not be on her.

But the sky felt too empty.

And the sea felt too full.

Once Nimbus found a comfortable place,
she sat until she was soaked through.

Then she took a deep breath, and
prepared to come face-to-face . . .

with the cloud.

Her cloud.

But this time, she tried something new.

The more Nimbus got to know her cloud,
the less she wanted to pretend it wasn't there.

Or run from it.

Or bottle it up.

Eventually, Nimbus felt ready to talk.
But she didn't know where she would find
someone who wanted to listen.

To her surprise, someone found *her*.

KELP?

The friends were excited to have found each other,
but they both felt a little unsure about where to begin.

So Nimbus took a deep breath, and introduced Kelp to her cloud.

The more Kelp got to know the cloud,

the more comfortable Nimbus became

with the idea of sharing it with him.

So comfortable that everything she had wanted to talk to her friend about finally burst forth.

It turned out, Kelp was a very good listener.

The friends took their time heading
back to the beach.
They talked about the sky, and the sea,
and how nervous Nimbus was to see
everyone again.

When they finally reached the shore,
Nimbus had butterflies in her stomach
and a cloud above her head.

But this time, she didn't
mind if everyone noticed.

Nimbus knew that some days would be all sunshine and rainbows,

and others would be a little more . . .

cloudy.

But maybe, just maybe . . .

those days would be better if
they were weathered together.